The Adventures of Martin Luther

Written by Carolyn Bergt
Illustrated by Art Kirchhoff

Concordia Publishing House

Copyright© 1999 Concordia Publishing House
3558 S. Jefferson Avenue, St. Louis, MO 63118-3968
Manufactured in the United States of America

All rights reserved. No part of this publication may be reproduced, stored in a retrieval system, or transmitted, in any form or by any means, electronic, mechanical, photocopying, recording, or otherwise, without the prior written permission of Concordia Publishing House.

Scripture taken from the HOLY BIBLE, NEW INTERNATIONAL VERSION®. NIV®. © 1973, 1978, 1984 by the International Bible Society. Used by permission of Zondervan Publishing House. All rights reserved.

3 4 5 6 7 8 9 10   08 07 06 05 04 03 02 01 00

Young Martin Luther lived long ago
In days of queens and of kings
With castles tall and knights flashing swords,
But none of our modern things.

With father Hans, a hard-working man,
And mother Margaret, too,
He lived in Germany far away
Across the ocean blue.

At school he sat on benches hard
And studied every day.
He laughed and sang like other kids do,
And on his lute he would play.

It may have been an exciting time,
Yet it was difficult, too.
Few people knew the gift of God's grace—
The love He gives me and you.

"A lawyer! That's what Martin should be."
Hans said, "My boy will be rich."
But watch and see, for God knows what's best,
As Luther's plans made a switch.

As Martin walked one day in the rain,
In woods outside of the town,
The lightning flashed and thunder crashed,
And Martin fell to the ground.

"God's mad at me! I fear that I'll die."
He cried, "St. Anne, save me now!
I'll give away my things to the poor,
And then I'll take a monk's vow."

Poor Martin still did not know the truth—
That God sees all of our tears,
But saints and angels can't answer prayer.
Our prayers reach only God's ears.

A monastery now was his home.
His bedroom was a small cell.
He knelt to pray each day seven times
Whenever called by the bell.

He hoped to earn God's love by His deeds.
He tried to be very good.
But total sinners—that's what we are.
We don't do things like we should.

Poor Martin felt he'd never be right.
His sins were such a disgrace.
He did not know that we are forgiv'n
By Christ, who's taken our place.

One day he read the Bible's Good News—
Forgiveness, heaven are free!
Christ Jesus died for us on the cross.
He gives us His victory!

So Luther wanted people to know—
God's gifts aren't something we do.
By faith in Christ we all can be saved.
God's Word tells us it is true!

Not all agreed and some turned away
Like Tetzel, who'd loudly sing:
"If you drop coins in this wooden chest—
A soul to heaven will spring."

Now Luther knew what had to be done.
The Scripture's truth must be heard.
So Luther wrote a list to debate,
All based on God's holy Word.

He nailed his list for people to see
Right on the church's front door.
His statements bold (in all, ninety-five)
Soon caused a mighty uproar.

The printing press made copies for all.
The people learned in each town:
The Lord hates sin, but loves you and me;
That's why to earth He came down.

For only Jesus lived perfectly
And then He died in our place.
By faith we know forgiveness is ours.
In heav'n we'll meet face to face.

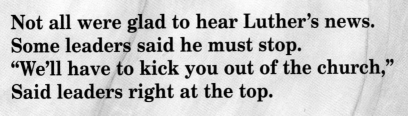

Not all were glad to hear Luther's news.
Some leaders said he must stop.
"We'll have to kick you out of the church,"
Said leaders right at the top.

But Martin did not listen to threats
Or what their letters might say.
He said, "The truth's in Scripture alone.
It's God whom I must obey."

He next was sent to court for a trial,
Accused, like liars and thieves.
The emperor watched, as lawyers declared,
"It's wrong what this man believes."

But Luther stood strong and would not recant.
The Spirit blessed him with *pow'r*.
He bravely spoke of God's gift of grace
In that remarkable hour.

He said, "Unless from God's holy Word
You show that my words are wrong,
I'll never stop, I'll never recant.
I trust the Lord, who is strong."

The emperor said, "This never will do!"
The court buzzed like a beehive.
"Leave town, outlaw, for I now decree:
You're wanted, dead or alive!"

Without a worry, Luther went home.
He knew the end of the story—
No matter what might happen that day,
It all would be for God's glory.

A rumbling noise disturbed Martin's ride.
A group of knights stopped his cart.
They kidnapped him and hurried away,
Escaping fast in the dark.

But what relief! The danger was gone.
The Wartburg was a safe place.
(Sir George was Luther, now in disguise,
A knight with a beard on his face.)

A year went by while Martin worked hard
Until all danger was clear.
He went back home to preach once again
Of Christ, our Savior most dear.

He only hoped to change what was wrong.
Reform was all that he planned.
He preached, he taught, he wrote many books
To help us all understand.

God blessed his life, and wife Katie's, too,
With six kids who loved the Lord.
They had good friends and good songs to sing.
"Praise God, our Savior, adored!"